LOCAL MUMBAI

VARDAN

SUMEET KUMAR

Copyright © Sumeet Kumar
All Rights Reserved.

This book has been self-published with all reasonable efforts taken to make the material error-free by the author. No part of this book shall be used, reproduced in any manner whatsoever without written permission from the author, except in the case of brief quotations embodied in critical articles and reviews.

The Author of this book is solely responsible and liable for its content including but not limited to the views, representations, descriptions, statements, information, opinions and references ["Content"]. The Content of this book shall not constitute or be construed or deemed to reflect the opinion or expression of the Publisher or Editor. Neither the Publisher nor Editor endorse or approve the Content of this book or guarantee the reliability, accuracy or completeness of the Content published herein and do not make any representations or warranties of any kind, express or implied, including but not limited to the implied warranties of merchantability, fitness for a particular purpose. The Publisher and Editor shall not be liable whatsoever for any errors, omissions, whether such errors or omissions result from negligence, accident, or any other cause or claims for loss or damages of any kind, including without limitation, indirect or consequential loss or damage arising out of use, inability to use, or about the reliability, accuracy or sufficiency of the information contained in this book.

Made with ♥ on the Notion Press Platform
www.notionpress.com

Sumeet Kumar

Sumeet Kumar , A adult who experiences many phases of life , a well known writer and a writer of new era . In reality he is a writter as well as singer (as a hobby) and a standup comedian . Very exciting and interesting fact about him is that he is author of New era i.e. he starts his journey of writing at the age when he was going to schools to get the study .His some famous works i.e. Maturity Of Love (Genre - Love),Privacy For Dream (Genre - Middle Class), Army Squad ofLove (Genre- The Seperation of Army Love), 5 Days of Love(Genre- Temporarily Love), Th e Endearment Of Love(Genre - Historical Era

Of Love), Social Destruction Indo-Pak (Genre - The Story of The Love At The Time Of Division Of India And Pakistan), Middle Class Soul (Genre - The Dreams of Middle Class), The Accursed Kanatpur (Genre -The Horrific Story Of A Village), Wrong Number (Genre -The Suspenseful Physco Killer Story), The Secrecy OfDeadly Midnight (Genre - The Suspense About a Crime),Fragile Religious Of Death (Genre- The Death Of A TrustfulPerson), Nature Vs Science (Genre - The Future Battle Between Nature And Science In A Horrific Way), Generic Man (Genre - The Dream of I.I.T), The Unconsious 12 Hours(Genre - The Illusion At Stage Of Comma), The StrangeBurden (Genre - The Burden Of Love) , Her Existence (Genre- The Female Pain In The Society) , Jockstrap Prize (Genre -The True Story Of A National Athlete) , H Man [Hindi] (Genre - Superhero Tragic Story), H Man [English] (Genre - Superhero Tragic Story) , Maturity Of Love [Englsih] (Genre - Love) and many more are available on various geners on the offcial platform of Amazon, Flipkart and Notionpress. You can buy them from there.

Contents

Contents

Preface

Life doesn't change because of someone's departure, but yes, the moments do change, which celebrate their moment Whom he doesn't deserve in our part Well, hatred increases love, but too much love makes people cry,this is just a story, a war of humanity against humanity,

Neither this story is of a hero nor that of a villain,This is the story of one who in his own part does not know what is his identity.

Acknowledgements

Sumeet Kumar

Sumeet Kumar , A adult who experiences many phases of life , a well known writer and a writer of new era . In reality he is a writter as well as singer (as a hobby) and a standup comedian . Very exciting and interesting fact about him is that he is author of New era i.e. he starts his journey of writing at the age when he was going to schools to get the study .His some famous works i.e. Maturity Of Love (Genre - Love),Privacy For Dream (Genre - Middle Class), Army Squad ofLove (Genre- The Seperation of Army Love), 5 Days of Love(Genre- Temporarily Love), Th e Endearment

ACKNOWLEDGEMENTS

Of Love(Genre - Historical Era Of Love), Social Destruction Indo-Pak (Genre - The Story of The Love At The Time Of Division Of India And Pakistan), Middle Class Soul (Genre - The Dreams of Middle Class), The Accursed Kanatpur (Genre -The Horrific Story Of A Village), Wrong Number (Genre -The Suspenseful Physco Killer Story), The Secrecy OfDeadly Midnight (Genre - The Suspense About a Crime),Fragile Religious Of Death (Genre- The Death Of A TrustfulPerson), Nature Vs Science (Genre - The Future Battle Between Nature And Science In A Horrific Way), Generic Man (Genre - The Dream of I.I.T), The Unconsious 12 Hours(Genre - The Illusion At Stage Of Comma), The StrangeBurden (Genre - The Burden Of Love) , Her Existence (Genre- The Female Pain In The Society) , Jockstrap Prize (Genre -The True Story Of A National Athlete) , H Man [Hindi] (Genre - Superhero Tragic Story), H Man [English] (Genre - Superhero Tragic Story) , Maturity Of Love [Englsih] (Genre - Love) and many more are available on various geners on the offcial platform of Amazon, Flipkart and Notionpress. You can buy them from there.

CHAPTER ONE

THE LOST SILENCE

Time is that lover of life who is not ready to come to everyone's side, we meet many people every day, we know about them, then we try to meet them many times, but sometimes we do not think whether they are true. It is necessary for us that we are unnecessarily working in front of them, some words get erased in speaking, but when those actions actually poison our lives, then we can understand its jewels, I have such relationships. Many We have seen that when the right time comes, they stay with us and are close to us by becoming our shadow, but when the face of time changes and it seems silent everywhere, then our relationship also shows its true like a blur, seeing which Every branch of our faith advises us to go away from him at that time. Well, I have seen time and faced many of it but today that feels that life is different from me, I have never been with someone.

Did not go against in his life, always kept his humanity attached to himself, loved him more than himself, that too lest the winds of love make me his partner, first used to think that it is very dangerous to be a good person, but now Ayesha feels that a bad person is more difficult than that,

CHAPTER TWO

TRIED TO FORGET HUMANITY

TRIED TO FORGET

I want to leave my good because my soul needs a new face, if God does not change the time, then move ahead and do not harm me by my nature and my thinking, I want to stop my own thinking I can't, even if she is wrong, but I feel she is my own, I wish to separate her from myself every day, because I know that if I come close to her, my relations will go away and eventually they will also stop. Can't find, on myself,

There is so much writing that now every print of paper has started trying to stay away from me, my silence also wants to go away from me, which had become my soul mate for me in n years, well I am not angry with anyone about this thing Why are they leaving with me?

There is only one thought that bothers me all the time, it breaks me from inside, I am not able to connect with him even after six months, I have also asked many questions to him that what do you want from me? But she doesn't even answer me in sex time, she doesn't want to take me away from her place, no matter how far I go from her, she always tries to come close to me, even in the shadow of sorrow, now she is the reason for my life. Change the city, these six houses will not change my destination.

CHAPTER THREE

CARE OF HELL

when people ask how are you? Thinking never wants me to be weak? If my happiness also comes in my lap, even if it is only for some time, still can't I paint in their colour? After all, why is this even a question of mine?

Someone's memories are still present in my mind, I don't try to separate them from myself, I do this every day, but now I have a tendency to lose in front of those relationships, who promised to be with me in a big gathering I don't even know how to get out of them, I want the freedom of two moments, which I am not getting in my share, I wish to run away somewhere far away, neither the community of humans nor dreams Army, I am so much from that God Can't even ask that my God release me from the world, not living in the roof, my soul which is yearning everyday, that too someone's memories, who is his fault?

Why are you making me a part of your God means the world, if freedom is written in my nature, then give me more freedom, because this life is now too painful than death, I want to sleep in that grave I want to make every single night like a bird that is free to fly within itself, it is not a matter of happiness that the troubles will not be there, but the way I fight with myself today and think of being free every day from my own place

I am trying to destroy it so that I can get freedom from it.

CHAPTER FOUR

THE JOURENY OF WEALTH

What have I lost in my life? Why should I tell this to someone else, and even if told, will they really be able to give me freedom inside me, they will go on ruining me further, trusting that wealth in life which cannot be given to everyone easily because of public This is the village of my life, if I get lost in its part, then after a time, I may never get success in it, when that God knows my condition, when that God knows my condition, whatever my religion.

Why don't I talk about how many parts, my God, my Allah, my God, the ones who have not changed at all, I understand the words of the books, I also know about them, but do they know my problems, how I I am controlling myself, do they know this? Whenever we need him, he is always there for us, I think that .

Now I don't have the courage to say that I can leave myself and move forward because I am not like that, my relationships have become my weakness. I will have to talk a little with myself, even though the destination is one, but there are two ways, if I choose one of these two, then maybe the other reason will be considered bad, and if there is time, I will not choose anyone in these don. My life will feel bad .

CHAPTER FIVE

ALTERED VIBE

I could not finish the journey that I have started, only people are not ruined in love and there are many things in this world which have been destroyed by a desire and attitude to ruin us, which we can see with our own eyes. It is possible, but we do not have the courage to separate it, after all, should I do it? Can't end the relationship of a year in one stroke, can't he tell them that I hate the feeling of your existence, every far away from you

Wants to stay away and safe too, maybe I don't have the courage to bear that pain which is never my own and will never be mine, then go away from me if possible because I want to live that too openly, I Don't be in bondage to anyone, I hate myself because of you, I don't consider myself strong, and with time I am also weak, neither can I accept you as my love, nor can you give me your happiness, strength and If you give silence in part, then that.

You won't be able to bear the feeling and say our relationship will never be strong after a while, well I didn't get any special love from anyone, but I can definitely say that his character of washing was amazing, Because I was following his false love as a matter of truth, it is not necessary for me to public, I also knew that if I give place to my part in it, then my happiness will go away from me and

Syed today's evening is the name of the same thing. .

CHAPTER SIX

ATTACHED WITH PAIN

Giving time to relationships means keeping them attached to yourself even more, not everyone understands this thing, the one who will leave your side in God's era will leave, I never believe in luck because it is a right of the people. The one who is present inside us since long, we can never separate her from ourselves, she stays with us all the time like a coming in our life and makes us aware of the reality of our relationship.

Childhood memories are so strong that we never forget them, but if we create fond memories in our youth, we always try to separate them from ourselves, to go away from them, why? Because the relationships that we are ignorant of are made by the thread of attachment and the relationships that we think in youth are made with understanding, their ties are as weak as them, I do not consider anyone as big, neither infatuation nor Only to think The thing is that childhood,these Egyptians stay away from adulteration with relationships, but they completely lose their identity in the adulteration of young relationships and they do not even realize that the one who is with them is not going to stay with them for a long time.

CHAPTER SEVEN

DESIRE OF WAR

Someone had said that it is better to learn something than try to make it your own, and that statement was wrong because when we make our relationships, we stop celebrating the time behind which each and every desire of ours is in it. It is very important, and maybe , about whom I am going to present every wish of his in front of all of you, which is related to his right, I feel very proud even today, maybe , the memories are not so bad.

It seems that she is not bad, she is very bad, just call it wasted, I have never asked for a chance to love me, she should try to touch me, we didn't meet before, we talked for a few days and then It takes a lot of hard work, but we all have a story, we give so much importance to that one witness, they give so much importance to that relationship that they become special for us even if they don't want to, my first love is just my ma's affection,And the second is my father's respect, but I neither have any desire for anything more than this, nor have I ever wished for anything more than this, well if I get confused in words, then time will pass and that witness Let the story not remain incomplete, Ishqiye, let me introduce you to such a traveler who used to give comfort to some people even among the silent adore of hug ....

WEALTH IS SATISFACTION

wealth, the only nature of a person can never stand, even if for some time he forgets the identity of the shape in his feeling, but his desire never allows him to do wrong, if the light of the lamp decreases in the house, then the blind At that time the silence of the whole house takes time within its illusion, but they say that there is no night for the sun and no morning for the moon, these two are very different from each other and their power is our world.

It is very important for them, yet both of them never forget their homes, maybe there is a reason for that too, if a witness is angry with you and he is very close to you, then at that time you felt your love for him, and you never lost that sorrow. Those who don't show what you feel every day, that too inside yourself, this world is heavy with vanity, there is more humanity than that in God's world, if you throw a stone at it, read thousands of prayers to get rid of its cold.

When God created us, he never made us thinking that we will be jealous and hate ourselves, when God created us, he made us thinking that I am making a human being We are their children, I heard this long time back, even today, they can never see us in trouble, but if they don't see us in trouble, they can't control our death within themselves, so what are those who have died? They can control their attitude,

I don't think because if not them then only we have been made, we ourselves play the role of slaughter, this role of killing a human being, has any god killed any human being till date? I don't think so? Because the temple we ask is also built by us, the shrine in front of which we bow our head, we also built it, so when we consider every wall of love as our own, then why don't we consider hatred?

CHAPTER NINE

HERO OR VILLIAN ?

If humans can be wrong, then it is also possible that the relationships made by them are wrong like them, I am not talking about that God, that God is still present in our body, but it means that Not that I forget my own role, forget my own humanity, I can take God's incomplete story on some other long journey, but the story of that witness should not remain incomplete; It's troubling me and I don't want to ruin someone's immortal story in such a godly way...

Mumbai Dharavi

(400017).......

Aditya Holkar ...

I want to tell about myself before putting each and every root of this story, I do not know how far the needle of my life is, its threads will try to keep me alive for a long time, but I have a desire to make a name in which I die. I don't want to forget my name, well you all make my name known.

CHAPTER TEN

ALIVE FOR MY MOTHER

Live,About whom some special memories are not attached, but yes, I get angry very quickly, talk about love in front of me. If it goes wrong, my saree can never be right, well let me tell about my father, I am an honest policeman, I have not taken any relationship with him till date, well his identity is Shrikant Holkar, except for the name he Till date neither has given anything to my mother (Aaee) nor to me, mine and her never make up neither does she respect me nor do she have a secret behind this too The story of

the secret of is related to my dreams and wealth Even in my childhood, whenever I used to tell the boys of the big house together, I love toys very much, so one day I tried to steal them and the same day my father saw me and told me Lentils in your treasure at that time I must have been 12 years old, but I was 26 years old, my Anandar, that day for the first time my father filed an FIR against me, then came to steal from my father's laughter and many scars in his childhood which were visible on his leather belt. The glory of I wanted to become a big man, I had big dreams of love, I never thought that what to do in life except earning money, I used to consider the locality as Taj Mahal, she was also unfaithful, just like my father's job, which used to give respect. There was but no happiness, I was fed up with my old life, I didn't have the interest to study since childhood, I also had the wealth to think of playing, but my father had trouble with us too, Ishqiye threw me out at the age of 17 like.

CHAPTER ELEVEN

GARBAGE BORN HUMAN

Some people throw the garbage outside, at that time when my father was taking me out of the locality, the whole world opened my eyes and the world was happy that day, but my mother's eyes were full of tears, but I could not see them. What would she have done, at that time she would have chosen her own son as her husband, if she had chosen me, my father would have been destitute, and even if she had not chosen, no one would have been destitute at that time, I have no harm to my father, but who He didn't, I swore humanity,She also killed that moon for the sake of wealth, which was not even hers, even though she was not respected, but she was mine, from that day she started to love and hate more, I had thought from that day that one day this much wealth would belong to Kalyug.

Complete (akkha) Mumbai will stay on my feet, love I thought to start some business, but I did not have that much money in my hands, because when my father took me out of his house, I had 60 rupees in my hand, and Along with the busyness of the world, his After leaving, I will say that he did not think about this even once, and I was already homesick, but the day my bao left, that day

Chhath's craving also started playing, and a different world of hunger and thirst. That day David went to Anna, but I knew this pain would also be tolerated in love . what is the caste of is david anna and this Some kind of animal, I had gone that day to ask for work from him, but he made me his right hand, at first I was very confused that has the direction of the sun changed today? And I have met Ish Takle a few days back, then why is he asking me without moonlight, that too a safe one, before I felt that I should refuse, but the poor does anything for hunger and at that time I No one was more poor in love, thought that it is better than dying on charity.

CHAPTER TWELVE

RIGHT SIDE OF INIQUITY

To be on its right side, David Anna used to trade flowers, which means in simple language, girls' taskery, but even I did not know this thing at that time, because he really used to do business of flowers, means my People will be so proud of the society that humans are one but their businesses are many, meaning in front of the world it was Ramesh Apte who is in the business of flowers, whereas in front of us is David Anna who does girls' taskery, when I helped him for the first time. His time had become his fan, now it is a shame to ask when did this happen?Well, let me share this with you too, when my father had thrown me out of the house, my life suffered two losses at that time, the first one was that I was thrown out of the house and the second one was that I destroyed Dawat Shinde's Daas cavity in celebration. Meaning I had said this to David Anna, but the matter was something else?

CHAPTER THIRTEEN

THE LESSON OF MAHABHARAT

THE LESOOAnd that too because of my father's honesty, because of which he had to give all the money I had earned to Daivat Shinde, my father put the same money in the government's pocket, that too for a copper medal, when this matter When Daivat Shinde came to know, he had sent goons after me to kill me, but I can't say whether my luck was good or bad, because when the road was cut, he used to take his steps for a short time because at that time Morning is not celebrated in our community,But I jumped my step and got trapped in such a world of David Anna, from where there were ways to get out, but they were very dangerous, I also miss maybe Ma's training, I can't even tell her that Ma (Come) I miss you a lot, because I had left the house, but the memories of him were still there, I could not get along with my father at all, the whole world knew that he should kill me, who knows what I told him. My father Shrikant Holkar

It was shown, it is said that if things remain in the house, then it is loyal even in its walls, and the air of honesty, which had become a boundary brtween me and my father, was very important to go away during those times, David Anna knew very well that how much I hate my father, I was careful before because I did not want to make an arrow that would become the reason for the defeat of my own house. This story was on that peacock from where neither can I return Nor can I reveal to anyone why I came here? My story is not as much as it seems because now it has a beginning which I write, well when there was no money in my pocket David Anna told me I was careful and could not go against him in love, because at that time it was not only about humanity, but about a debt that I had got because of my father, I knew that I was supporting the wrong, then I did not back my hands. Could, I Mahabharata at that time.Nor can I reveal to anyone why I came here? My story is not as much as it seems because now it has a beginning which I write, well when there was no money in my pocket David Anna told me I was careful and could not go against him in love, because at that time it was not only about humanity, but about a debt that I had got because of my father, I knew that I was supporting the wrong, then I did not back my hands. Could, I Mahabharata at that time......

CHAPTER FOURTEEN

FRIDAY

Date: 22/04/2005

Day : Friday

There are two types of wealth in life, which is the desire of every person, whether he is poor or rich, this one is brought up in the abuses of garbage, this one is in the gutter, this one is in a big building, it is known as The first two are our sweethearts, which we call money, and on which Bapu's photo with a cool smile is pasted, looks like a green leaf and when it comes in the pocket, it gives peace, and the second sweetheart is a little bitch for decent people. because he works hard in his era , She does it, but people love her equally, well, her name is known and respected, who has both of these, that person sometimes wins even after doing everything, and he has all the wealth of the world. In my mind, I was the first wealth in him, but the second was very far away from my him, and I never get it, I never worked that hard to get it. Per that wealth was in my father's share and it was also uncountable, both of us they were very different from each other, Shrikant Holkar like people are not wrong, the whole world says that even my mother, but if I talk about myself in the same place, then the whole world thinks I am wrong, in my condition I myself knew that I was in some unconscious state. I am singing my life but I never want to bow down to anyone, I neither wanted to become the king of Mumbai nor to rule it, I just don't want the glory of that slap husband, even though I was not born in palaces I am definitely a king Will be made, and there is an evening behind it too, which will be few words to say, so this evening is of 24th April, the day my father took me out of his house, but on that day another thing happened which only I know. Yes, that day my father had brought down my respect but there was someone else who had done this, she was not close to me but I believed everything in her, I would have been careful that day if I wanted to, but it was a coincidence that my luck was not with me. Nor was his love pure for me, I had heard the time.

People change with people, but his love changed only after seeing my time, yes, I agree that I had done many wrong things, but I did not say the crime for which I was punished that day, if I had told an incomplete story Even the story of my crime could not understand my justice in it, that,s why let's tell from the beginning.

CHAPTER FIFTEEN

WARNING MEMORIES

April 24, this day in which even six of us cannot forget, it is said that there is no place for religion in love, but it was in my favor and the initials of her name were "Afreen Hafiza" which was my only ruin and my love. People are often ruined in love and settled too, but in my part both of these were found at the same time, means Afreen came in my life when I lost myself, which was such a big waste in me at that time. not far from my own self

I can do it, danceable is not even taking the name of going away from me, I was not able to control myself, it was such a thing, my father never let me become what I wanted to be, the feast of books killed my childhood first but When I grew up, my father's taunts took its place, I don't know what I wanted to make, but I don't want to make Imran like my father, I met Afreen the other night, and that night was so intoxicating that he Every day but even today make me son

When we met, we were completely unknown to each other, but the day I saw her, I had lost everything, even though I could see only her eyes in the burqa, but her,The eyes were also not an issue with the moon, but it is said that there are many spots in a moon, some are good and some are bad, and in my part they were both, it is said that when a person gets used to something If it is there, it can never be removed from its place, and I think Afreen has become the same for me, when I saw her for the first time that day, I do not know at all that what is there in her? I mean, even if I can break a person's 32 days, in front of him.

CHAPTER SIXTEEN

ROAD GANG FIGHT

Maybe it was not possible for me to tell about my love at that time, but before I took my step for him, there were some dogs who had to tell their status, Ishqiye na that day, my fight with the road gang in dushere I don't know why the untoward incident did not mess with me, because when I was looking at Afreen, at that time a member of the road gang tried to hit me with a hockey stick.

She is also lying on the same ground with my saree, it is said that people fall madly in love, but that day he was about to go blind for the first time, before that he would have killed me, I had already given him to Gandhi Hospital. , So Syed 56 will come, that too after meeting everyone and 1084 bones were broken, including all of them, it is said that every boy in black clothes is not wrong, and in white clothes, every person is not ready to die, that day everything was going well. If their people told me ours

If I had done it, I would have lost my love letter before, before that she was lost in her community, but says that if destiny is destined to destroy, even erasing her handwriting does not change her dreams, and maybe my meeting in her community Even though there swas a problem for him on one side, but for me he was in my first love, we were in the second time, this time the situation was very different from before, because this time we were directly on my father's post, means behind the bars.

CHAPTER SEVENTEEN

SENSE WITH TOUCH

Because I once again crossed someone's limits. But I could not understand at that time that I had come out from the city of that advice, I was imprisoned behind the bars, then later it came to know that the way I broke the bones, it turned out to be my only year, meaning Shadab Hafiz Khan, per Even at that time, her eyes were not rising towards me for hatred, Sayyid Udi time should understand that this is not love, it is for me, I knew that I am not capable of love, because whose father never accepted his only sons as his own, did he not have any love for himself?

For a few moments on the way from a very stranger, I could not understand at that time what my life wanted from me? Neither the wealth in his share nor the wealth of the father, whatever else he can never set his mind on, a mother who has full faith in her son that he will definitely change one day, and there is a soul that can change me. This is not the request of my mind by foot.

CHAPTER EIGHTEEN

DEAD FACE

That day, when she had come to pick up her brother, she did not even complain against me, that too even after my father told her, I even told her that I am not afraid to do it, but That day her silence revealed something and said everything, there was love in her eyes for my destruction name, when I got ruined that day, I really lost my senses this time, when my father called me two days after that day.

Lock that too outside the house and leave it on terrace he was also hungry and thirsty, and mother was also refused to come close to me, and had also given many oaths that if you feed her, if she tries to lose her bond, Kaveri will see my dead face.....

KAVERI HOLKAR

Kaveri Holkar who came to my whole world and my mother also (came), well I didn't know that I belong to her father, she came to my locality a few days back, and her sister whom I have fallen in love with is in the house below me. Live only, well live anywhere? That day when my father had tied me up but left me to die, then she came with food for me and told her that?

CHAPTER TWENTY

SYILL BROKEN BUT STABLE

Aditya: Oh yours, you are doing this, that too my shell and your brother's bones are still broken.

Afreen: She will join in a few days but I don't think yours is going to join..

Aditya: The God who breaks my bones is not born in the world, but yes, the day I am released from the bondage of my father, I will worship everyone on that day.

Afreen: Good! Everyone's argument will be done later Mr. First eat food..

Aditya: You have started eating food for me while I beat your brother, still I am not dreaming anywhere, complete Mumbai hates me and you have started eating food for me, are you acting good? That, and if poison comes out somewhere in it to drip on me, don't worry, you are not going to die in Bhidu because you have a special bonding with Yamraj..

Afreen: Yours is done, and listen Mr. whoever you are, I know that my brother had made a mistake this time in love,

I came to say sorry to him and I don't want to listen to your nonsense, you will be a don in your eyes. But in my eyes you are a human being love for the sake of Allah don't do these things and eat..

CHAPTER TWENTY-ONE

THE LOVE OF ANGEL

Aditya: Take it away, I don't want to eat and there is no need for my kindness, brother-in-law, till date my father has not accepted me as a human being and you are giving me knowledge, come on..

Afreen: Do you eat or not if I force you to do so anyway your eight legs are tied, you can't even do anything right now.

Aditya: At least show me your hand..

Afreen: Ok wait you..

CHAPTER TWENTY-TWO

LESSON ABOUT HUMOR ?

That day maybe for the first time I lost my victory in front of her love, I could not do anything when she was feeding me against me with her own hands, had become her prisoner, and Syed was also a free bird in her love. My eyes were very bent, I wanted to do it in front of him, but I was afraid of not denying it,that stone heart doesn,t feel any kind of pain , and anyway, such a thing like respect does not suit my love for him, after all this, he opened his hands and killed me. so much that

Even though I am unknown to you, but you have become my whole world for me and after today neither my hand in front of me can even take my life, have we met before? These are the things of my place, I mean at that time I was questioning myself that why is the unknown girl celebrating me so much? And why did I go so weak in front of him? Has she come forward in the form of humanity?

RELIEF

*"HER MEMORIES
DON'T EVEN
TOUCH MY SOUL
TILL MORNING
BUT OFTEN AT
NIGHT SHE RUINS
ME ."*

FORGET MY CHARM

"EVEN YOU
GIVE
YOUR LIFE
FOR SOME
PEOPLE
THEY WILL
NOT UNDERSTAND
YOUR CARE."

www.ingramcontent.com/pod-product-compliance
Lightning Source LLC
Chambersburg PA
CBHW020516160726

47991CB00007B/2981